Baby Penguins Everywhere!

This book is for Holly

Baby Penguins Everywhere!

Melissa Guion

PHILOMEL BOOKS ○ An Imprint of Penguin Group (USA) Inc.

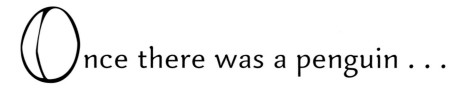

Once there was a penguin . . .

who was all alone.

She enjoyed the peace and quiet
of the sea and ice. Yet some days . . .

she felt lonely.

One day, she saw something
floating in the water . . .

a hat.

And from that hat popped

a little penguin!

And another!

The penguin was happy for the company.

But then came another.

And another
and another and
another.

There were baby penguins everywhere.

Now the penguin
wasn't lonely anymore.

She was very,
very busy.

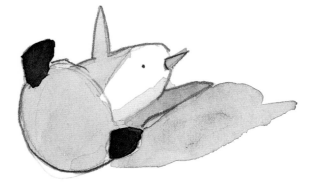

And more than a bit tired.

Happy as she was,

she needed something.

Just a minute to herself.

Because we all need
some time to be alone . . .

though being together . . .

is a lot more fun!

PHILOMEL BOOKS

A division of Penguin Young Readers Group.   Published by The Penguin Group.
Penguin Group (USA) Inc., 375 Hudson Street, New York, NY 10014, U.S.A.

Penguin Group (Canada), 90 Eglinton Avenue East, Suite 700, Toronto, Ontario M4P 2Y3, Canada (a division of Pearson Penguin Canada Inc.).   Penguin Books Ltd, 80 Strand, London WC2R 0RL, England.   Penguin Ireland, 25 St. Stephen's Green, Dublin 2, Ireland (a division of Penguin Books Ltd).   Penguin Group (Australia), 250 Camberwell Road, Camberwell, Victoria 3124, Australia (a division of Pearson Australia Group Pty Ltd).   Penguin Books India Pvt Ltd, 11 Community Centre, Panchsheel Park, New Delhi - 110 017, India.   Penguin Group (NZ), 67 Apollo Drive, Rosedale, Auckland 0632, New Zealand (a division of Pearson New Zealand Ltd).   Penguin Books (South Africa) (Pty) Ltd, 24 Sturdee Avenue, Rosebank, Johannesburg 2196, South Africa.   Penguin Books Ltd, Registered Offices: 80 Strand, London WC2R 0RL, England.

Published simultaneously in Canada. Manufactured in China by South China Printing Co. Ltd.
Edited by Michael Green.   Design by Semadar Megged.   Text set in 22-point Veronika LT Std.
The illustrations are rendered in watercolor and pencil.

Library of Congress Cataloging-in-Publication Data
Guion, Melissa.   Baby penguins everywhere / Melissa Guion.   p. cm.   Summary: "When a penguin finds a hat floating by, she discovers something inside . . . baby penguins!"—Provided by publisher.   [1. Penguins—Fiction. 2. Animals—Infancy—Fiction.] I. Title.   PZ7.G9434Bab 2012   [E]—dc23   2012002318

ISBN 978-0-399-25535-9

1 3 5 7 9 10 8 6 4 2